One Cool Friend

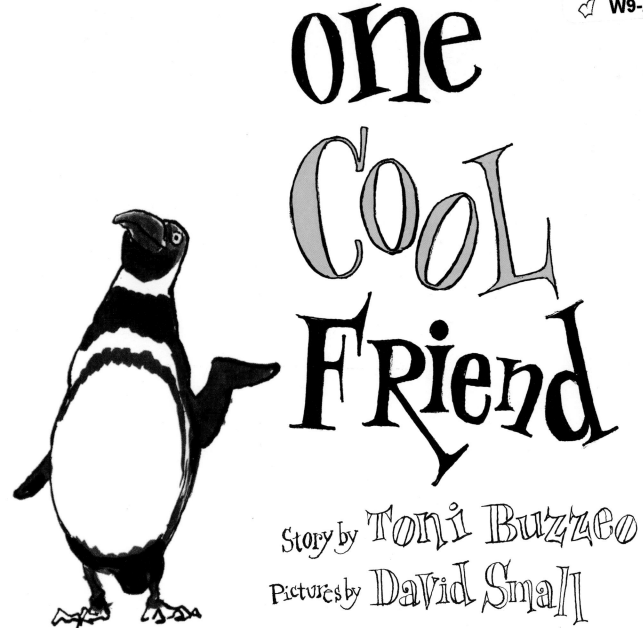

Story by Toni Buzzeo

Pictures by David Small

SCHOLASTIC INC.

For Ms. Joanne Stanbridge, one cool and unblinking friend,

whose love and laughter brought Magellan to his full glory —TB

To Edison —DS

ISBN 978-0-545-68395-1

12 11 10 9 8 7 6 5 4 3 2 1   14 15 16 17 18 19/0

Printed in the U.S.A.   40

First Scholastic printing, January 2014

Designed by Lily Malcom
Text set in Stone Informal
The art was done with pen and ink, ink wash, watercolor, and colored pencil.

Elliot was a very proper young man.

So on Saturday morning when his father said,

"Family Fun Day at the aquarium. Shall we go?"

Elliot thought, *Kids, masses of noisy kids.* But he only said,

"Of course. Thank you for inviting me."

At the aquarium, Elliot's father settled on
a bench to read his *National Geographic*.

"Have some fun, Elliot," he said.

So Elliot did.

He skipped the mobs of kids at the Giant Saltwater Tank,
Amazing Jellies Display, and Hands-on Tide Pool Exhibit.

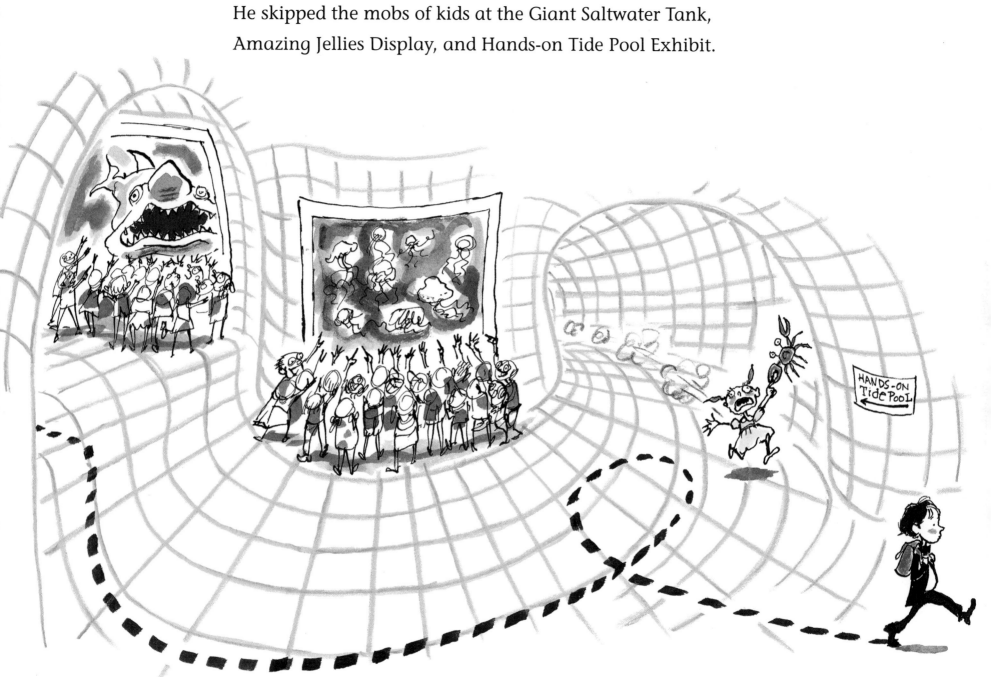

HANDS-ON
TIDE POOL
←

At the end of the hall, he discovered . . .

PENGUINS!

In their tidy black feather tuxedos with their proper posture, they reminded Elliot of himself.

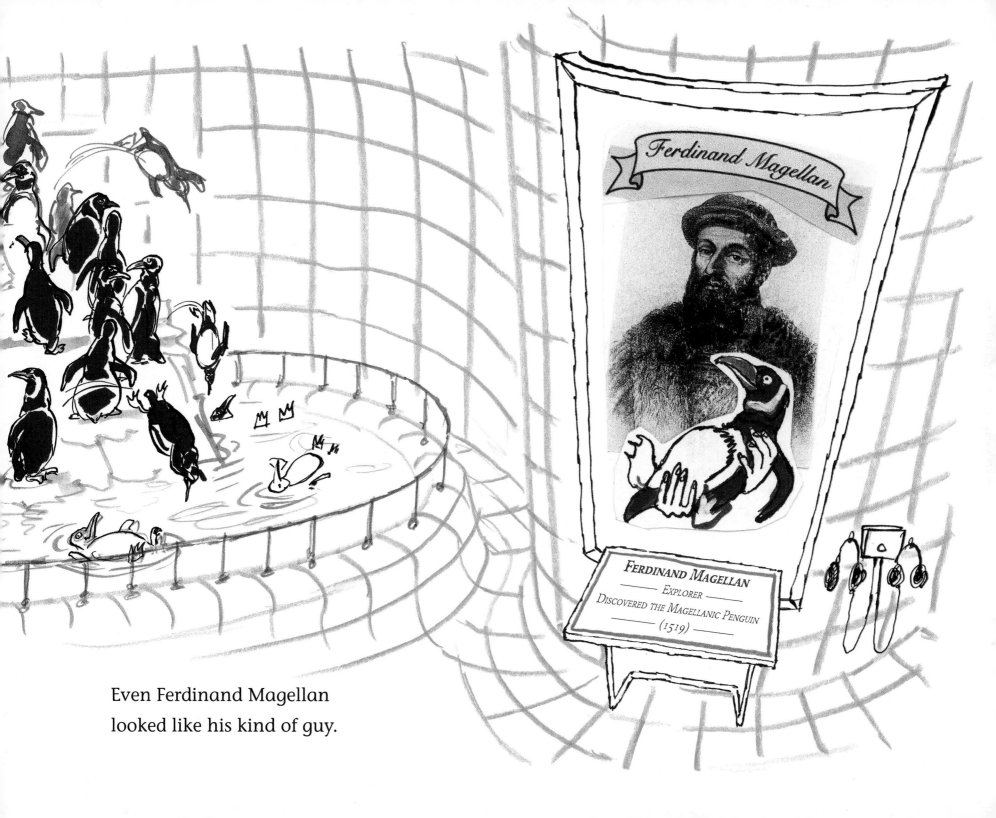

Even Ferdinand Magellan
looked like his kind of guy.

Ferdinand Magellan

FERDINAND MAGELLAN
— EXPLORER —
DISCOVERED THE MAGELLANIC PENGUIN
(1519)

Elliot emptied the school notices from his backpack,
selected the smallest penguin,

and popped it inside.

In his room, Elliot dialed the air conditioner down to its coldest setting.

"Maybe you'd like to skate?" Elliot asked.

"Grock!" said Magellan.

So Elliot dragged his old wading pool upstairs, then fed the garden hose through the kitchen window and turned on the faucet.

HMS. BEAGLE

Soon the air conditioner had done its work.

Later, Elliot knocked on the door of his father's office.

"I have some research to do at the library about Magellan."

"When I was in third grade, I got Captain Cook," his father said.

"Where did you keep him?" Elliot asked.

But his father had already returned to charting the changing boundaries of the Great Barrier Reef.

Elliot and Magellan rode to the library.
When Elliot set him on the librarian's desk,
Magellan held completely still.
Ms. Stanbridge didn't blink an eye—even when
Magellan blinked his.

She helped them access www.PenguinsOnIce.com,
copy pages from *Antarctic Anecdotes*, and borrow
Best Behavior for Birds.

On the way home, Elliot stopped for eight bags of
ice and a snack. Luckily his father's twenty-dollar
bill was just enough to cover it.

Elliot read his library book aloud while Magellan cooled down. They shared a bag of Goldfish crackers, but Magellan was still hungry.

"May I please bake frozen pizzas for supper?" Elliot asked.

"That's nice of you," his father said.

"But the only flavor we have left is anchovy."

"Perfect," Elliot said. "Magellan loves them."

That evening, Elliot heard his father rummaging for ice cream.
Luckily, Magellan had politely moved the carton to the front of
the freezer shelf.

Unfortunately, Magellan forgot
his manners overnight.

When Magellan awoke he was longing for a swim.

Elliot drew him a deep tub of cold water.

He left Magellan diving and holding his breath.

Elliot rushed to the door.